## Also by Briony Collins

*Blame it on Me* (Broken Sleep Books, 2021)

# ALL THAT GLISTERS

*Collins*

ISBN: 978-1-915079-13-8

Cover design by Aaron Kent

Edited & Typeset by Aaron Kent

Broken Sleep Books (2022)

Broken Sleep Books Ltd
Rhydwen,
Talgarreg,
SA44 4HB
Wales

# *Contents*

# All That Glisters

Briony Collins

# ALL THAT GLISTERS

**AND** then it was Sullivan's turn to toss a fistful of dirt over the coffin. It was a gesture he never understood, but nonetheless tried his best to do well. Too soft a throw and he would appear bored, uncaring, but too hard and the margins for perceived animosity would split wide open. He had to get it right. There was a trick to it that people never talked about, a rolling in the wrist until the palm was turned up to the low sky which cracked between clouds. The earth tumbled free between his fingers. It sounded like rain on mahogany.

He didn't stay for the reception, instead popping up his umbrella and beginning the slow walk back to the train station. There was a time when Sullivan felt obliged to stay with a bereaved family until most people had gone home, but not for a little while now. Not for six months. When he stepped past the cemetery gates, he gave a single, wistful look back to the crowd gathering into the church for finger sandwiches. His stomach piped up at the thought. There was something about miniature versions of regular food that made them taste better, as if all the notes of a meal could play more delightfully upon the tongue in smaller quantities. Fumbling around in his blazer pocket, Sullivan worked his finger inside an open bag of chocolate eclairs and pulled one out. Using his teeth to pinch one end of the wrapper, he tugged it and it spun around in a blur of purple just below his range of vision. It was a poor substitute for Mrs Harrison's cream cheese and smoked salmon on white bread.

9

If his wife were with him, she'd tut and shake her head.

"You know those things are bad for your teeth," she'd say.

"I know, dear, but the Devil makes temptation easy and I'm a weak man." Then he'd grin and grab her waist.

"Sully! You have the appetite of a Labrador."

That was her favourite phrase. Every time he snacked between meals or went back for seconds, she told him he was behaving like a Labrador, but she'd say it with half-smile. The coy upturning of her mouth was always on the side facing away from him to hide her amusement, though he knew full well it was there and would wink in reply. After fifty years of marriage, they were bilingual; they spoke their native language and a special, coded one just for themselves.

His shoe came down in a puddle. It was just deep enough that the cold, grey water poured in over the top of his brown brogue and seeped into his argyle sock to his already numb toes beneath. Never had Sullivan wanted so desperately to be on a train, crammed into his seat next to a random, warm stranger, hurtling homeward across the drumming of steel rods. He let the remainder of the eclair slide down his throat and freed another one from the bag in his pocket. *Labrador indeed*, he thought as he popped his second sweet into his mouth. He rounded the corner and went straight through the station entrance.

The train journey was only forty-five minutes, followed by a ten minute walk. As long as there were no delays – *not bloody likely* – he'd be home within the hour. At least he was now under the cover of the station roof. Reading the screen that counted down to his train's arrival, he lowered his umbrella and shook it, before putting it into a carrier bag he'd stuffed into a pocket. Standing on the platform, Sullivan didn't see much point in searching for a spare bench upon which to park himself for the next couple of minutes – *thank God it was on time* – so instead he kept his eyes trained on the billboard behind the adjacent platform.

The woman on the advert was lifting her baby into the air, whose gleeful smile topped a chin coated in saliva and a crusting orange purée. While he sincerely believed that children were the most precious gift in the world, there was a secret he carried around since his own son, Quinn, was born; nothing was as off-putting as the bubbling, slurping mess an infant made as it ate. It was a conclusion that gathered supporting evidence over the years as Quinn grew up and moved from milk to mush. In fact, every time Sullivan ate ice cream for decades now, he couldn't help but think of Quinn's first.

Two years old was certainly too young for mini-golf, but that was the wonderful part of being a parent. Sullivan and Darleen could take little Quinn anywhere they wanted and tell people it was all for their son. They watched cartoons again, went into toy shops and played, even went to fun fairs and carnivals. Now it was mini-golf. Of course, it wasn't entirely selfish. Darleen read that children have much to gain from exposing them to lots of experiences early on – *'stimulating' was the word* – but they'd be lying if they said that it wasn't for their own enjoyment too.

After an hour of playing the course, the sun was beginning to overpower them and ice cream started to sound like the greatest idea in the world. Darleen took Quinn over to an empty field opposite to sit while Sullivan queued at the ice cream van. Over his shoulder, he watched her fan out her blue dress to the side and smooth it down, so Quinn could sit on top of it instead of directly on the grass. It was the same dress

Sullivan had given her five birthdays ago and was in pristine condition, but that was typical of Darleen. She never threw out anything if it could still be saved and always took care of everyone. She wrapped an arm around Quinn and placed her hand across his tummy to support him as he leaned against her. Using her free arm to reach into their bag, she pulled out a bottle of milk and brought it up to Quinn's lips.

On his way back to them, Sullivan couldn't help but smile. The wind changed direction and brought Darleen's hair around her face and into her eyes so she couldn't see anything. It always happened and her frustration made Sullivan chuckle. In the seconds before she was able to push her hair away, Sullivan darted around behind them and tip-toed deftly, sneaking up for the perfect scare.

"Raaa!" he said as he grabbed her from behind and she shrieked.

"Sully! Jesus. Come up behind a woman alone with her baby, why don't you? That's a good way to get your eyes scratched out!"

"Come now, I've brought an icy-cold treat to placate you."

She narrowed her eyes but couldn't supress her smile as she took her ice cream from him.

"Is it working?" Sullivan asked.

"Perhaps..." she said, licking the side. Raspberry. Her favourite. "Okay. Yes. Thank you, my love. And what flavour did you get? Let me guess –"

"– Vanilla," they said together.

"It's the best one," Sullivan said.

"Best one? Don't be absurd. Vanilla isn't a proper flavour. It's the complete absence of flavour! That's the point."

"What about when you put vanilla extract in your fairy cakes? That's a flavour."

"Well…that's different, it's –"

"– oh, honey, you might want to…err…" Sullivan interrupted, pointing at her ice cream.

She turned her head to find that half of it was missing. Quinn was grinning madly beneath a pink, dripping moustache.

"Oh, you like Mummy's ice cream, do you, you little devil?" Darleen said with feigned annoyance.

Quinn giggled and leaned in for more.

Sullivan blinked as the train pulled up to the platform. His toes squelched in his damp sock as he stepped up into the carriage and made his way through the aisle, searching for a place to sit. There was only one space available that he could see. A young woman sat in the window seat on her own, staring out at the same billboard.

"Excuse me, would you mind if I sat here?" he asked.

"Not at all, please," she said, gesturing that he was welcome.

Trains were different than he remembered them growing up. People didn't often ask about seats or chatter any more. Everyone liked to keep to themselves, plugged into their phones or with eyes glued to the backs of headrests. All passengers had a laser focus on where they were going or when they'd be free of the horrors of public transport. It was as though they didn't really see each other. Sullivan felt like he was the only person on board.

As discreetly as he could, he glanced at the woman next to him. She was wearing a navy blue suit with a lilac blouse and her long, black hair was pulled back into a single plait.

Her nails were painted pink, but she was using her left thumb to pick the polish off her right one, leaving chips of colour scattered across her table. Sullivan raised his eyebrows but didn't say anything, instead reaching into the inside pocket of his blazer. He pulled out a copy of *To Kill a Mockingbird* which he started to read on the train to the funeral earlier that afternoon. He felt a pair of eyes settle on him and looked up just in time to see the woman staring, before she abashedly smiled.

"Sorry. It's just I – I love that book," she said.

"Not to worry. I've only just started it. Always time to pick up a classic, eh?"

"That's what I think too."

"Not much in the way of mockingbirds thus far," he smiled. A man came down the aisle pushing a cart of refreshments. "I'm going to have a tea, I think," Sullivan said. "Would you like one?"

"Oh, it's okay."

"Nonsense, you seem to have something on your mind," he said, gesturing to her fidgeting hands. "Nothing a hot tea on a rainy day can't ease. How about this, I'll get two and if you want one, you can take it?"

The man set a tea down in front of the woman and handed the second to Sullivan. She nodded to herself as though making a decision.

"Thank you. Really. I've not been having the best day."

"It's no trouble. Here, there's some packets of sugar, should you –"

"I like mine without."

"Me too," Sullivan said.

Her phone began to ring from deep inside her handbag. Frantically, she clawed her way inside it and grabbed the device, barely tapping the 'answer' icon before bringing it up to her ear.

"Hello…yes, I'm on the train now…oh…oh, right…I see… not to worry…tomorrow is great…yes…okay, thanks…bye."

She dropped the phone back into her bag and took a long gulp from her tea, though Sullivan was sure it would still be too hot. Then she set the cup down with a thud and went back to scratching the paint off her nails.

"Mockingbirds really are fascinating creatures. Did you know they can recognise individual people? They're remarkable," Sullivan said.

"What?"

"Oh yes. Amazing animals. I once had a friend, Roger – what was his last name? It's on the tip of my tongue…Roger… Summers…no, that's not it…Ssssss – never mind, it doesn't matter. Anyway, Roger moved out to North America with his wife and while they were out there they got a dog.

"They had a routine with this dog. They always took it out before they fed it dinner when Roger got home from work, so it could have a wee in the yard. Lovely big yard, they had, with a huge tree growing in a back corner. One evening, the dog started to behave very strangely. It used to always want to stay out and play, roll around in the sunlight, grab sticks… you know, dog stuff.

"One night, it went out to wee and immediately turned around and began scratching at the door. Didn't even go to the toilet. Just doubled back straight away. It kept doing this night after night for about a week."

"What was wrong?" the woman asked.

"Well, that's where it gets really odd. See, Roger – Somerset! His name was Roger *Somerset*! Oh…er…sorry. So

Roger decided to take the little devil to the vet to see if there was something wrong medically. Dogs are usually pretty good at telling their owners when something isn't right, you know. The vet said not only was the dog fine, but it was the picture of perfect health! Roger couldn't make heads or tails of it…no pun intended.

"He took the poor dog home and told his wife. A few nights later, Roger and his wife were sitting out on their back deck, watching the sunset and waiting for the fireflies to come out, when they heard something that gave them a terrible shock. They would have sworn it was imaginary had they not both heard it at the exact same time."

"What was it?" the woman asked, now leaning towards Sullivan.

*"It was the dog's name."*

"No way!"

"Yes! Roger and his wife both heard another voice say their dog's name. Then they heard it a second time and that was when the dog inside started going mad. It was sitting inside behind a screen door, so it could hear everything perfectly. As soon as it heard its name, it began barking, trying desperately to get to its owners.

"Roger couldn't be sure, but he swore he heard the voice come from the big tree at the back of the yard. As his wife stood up to go inside and calm the dog down, a bird flew from the branches. He didn't get a good look at it, as it was only a silhouette against the sunset, but he did see how long its tail was. Now, Roger wasn't an irrational man. He knew that improbable didn't mean impossible, so he began to look up types of birds at the library the next day. And what do you think he discovered?"

"What?"

"Well, Roger found out that," Sullivan paused to take a deliberately long drink of tea, "mockingbirds are capable of imitating human speech."

"Wait, seriously?"

"Seriously. This mockingbird had learned to recognise Roger. And what do you suppose it always heard Roger call?"

"The dog's name?"

"The dog's name! Every single evening, Roger stepped into the garden and after a few moments would call the dog in for dinner. So the mockingbird began to associate the name with Roger and started to call it whenever it saw him. The dog knew it was about time for food, so –"

"So it turned around and went inside, thinking it was being called in to eat!" the woman said.

"Precisely. The mockingbird called the dog's name upon seeing Roger, making the dog think he was being called in for dinner. Could you believe it?"

"What did he do about it?" the woman asked, finishing her tea without taking her eyes off Sullivan for a second.

"There wasn't a great deal that could be done. Cutting down the tree, trying to get rid of the bird, changing the dog's name…none were very good options. In the end, Roger stopped going out with the dog altogether. He had to hide in his own house from a damned bird!" Sullivan chortled.

"That's incredible."

"Isn't it just? But I swear to you, there's not a word of a lie in the story. Mockingbirds are marvellous little rascals, I tell you."

They grinned at each other and Sullivan downed the last of his tea. Roger and that blasted bird was his favourite story to tell. It never failed to make the listener smile. He and Darleen still broke into peals of laughter decades after first reading the events in a letter from Roger in the late seventies. Darleen had to crouch down on the kitchen floor, bent double from fits of giggles that overtook her entire body, and tears slid down Sullivan's cheeks. Quinn walked in on the pair barely able to breathe from joy and couldn't help but chuckle at the sight of them. Soon all three were cackling uncontrollably.

"My name is Lupita," the woman said, bringing him back into the train carriage.

"Sullivan."

"That's a nice name. Unique."

"Thank you. As is yours. Took me a long time to like my own name."

"Why's that?"

"Well, with a name like Sullivan Protest you learn not to speak up too much in school. 'Sullivan doth protest too much' and the like. Grown-ups have no idea how much hold they have over children's minds sometimes, I think."

"I hear that," Lupita said.

The last of her nail polish on her thumb came free and she moved onto her first finger, clawing at the pink paint like Roger's dog at the door.

Darleen liked to paint her nails too. Sullivan often went on trips away with his best friend, Jonesy. On the return drives home, he made it his mission to scout out a purveyor of cosmetics and stop off to buy his wife a new bottle. It was always a fresh colour.

"I won't stop until you own every hue visible to the human eye. You'll have rainbows, darling. Rainbows," he said.

It seemed peculiar to Sullivan that he had a best friend at all. Some phrases don't age well and, as the decades went on, it became sillier in his mind that he could use the words "best friend" in earnest. Heath Jones was as close to the concept as he could get in his later years. It was Darleen's idea that he should talk to Jonesy in the first place, at his inaugural Christmas party with the town council.

"I can't be your best friend; I'm your *wife*," she said.

"So what? You can be both."

"Wife supersedes best friend, I'm afraid. I don't gain anything extra from being your pal when I'm already your soulmate. So get in there and go make a friend!"

Then she gave him a slight push through the doors to the venue. It was packed with faces he'd never seen before. Moving to a new town uprooted not only his life, but his sense of himself. Sullivan found it difficult to navigate the waters of starting over. Darleen stuck to the edge of the crowd, making a beeline for the mini sausage rolls, and Sullivan knew she would stay there until he began to socialise. There was no putting it off. Jonesy was the first person he saw, guffawing over what Sullivan presumed to be a terrible Christmas cracker joke, as no one else was laughing.

"Here, new fella," Jonesy said when he saw Sullivan approaching, "what do you call a chicken in a shell suit?"

"I don't know…"

"An *egg*," he said and began to howl with laughter again.

"That's…uhh…that's not funny."

"Of course it's not funny! Have you ever heard something so shit?"

They roared together. Best friends in the making. After New Year's, they went on their first trip together to York for a weekend. Darleen didn't want to go. She'd be bored stiff spending all of Saturday in the train museum like Sullivan and Jonesy planned. Thus, a tradition was born for the two friends and a new one was formed for Sullivan and Darleen.

On the journey home, an urge hit him. He didn't want to return empty-handed. It was nonsensical, of course, to want to bring an offering back to *his* house, but it was the first time he'd spent a night away from Darleen during their marriage. The snoring of Jonesy in the adjacent twin bed was an ill-replacement for the warmth of his wife's breath on his chest as she slept.

"Here, take the next exit," Sullivan said to Jonesy, who was driving.

"No, no, ours isn't for another hour."

"I want to find something for Darleen."

"Now, Sully, I know you're no Burt Reynolds but I'm sure your homecoming is enough for her. Come on, we need to make good time. If we stop, I'll be late dropping you off."

"Then we'd better make sure I have something on hand to convince my wife to forgive you."

Jonesy rolled his eyes and then cracked a smile. Without speaking, he flipped the indicator and switched lanes, pulling off the motorway at the next exit.

"Thank you," Sullivan said.

"Oh, don't you dare. This is for Darleen. Sweet as daises and cute as a button, but I don't doubt she's lethal."

They laughed as Sullivan turned the radio up a little louder and the two cruised around the strange town to the sound of Little Richard.

Lupita's phone rang again and Sullivan jumped. He was still half an hour away from being able to get off the train. For a second, he half-expected to see Jonesy sitting next to him, until he heard Lupita grumbling to herself as she grabbed her phone, saw who was calling, and put it away again without answering it. It buzzed and beeped inside her bag for thirty seconds and then was silent again. As it stopped, Lupita sighed.

"Avoiding someone?" Sullivan asked.

"No. I mean, yes. Maybe. I – I don't actually know."

She brushed the chips of nail polish off the table and smoothed out her jacket.

"It's my mum," she said. "It's terrible to avoid your mum, I know, but…there's just a lot on my mind and sometimes she can make things worse."

"It's never terrible to go easy on yourself when you have plenty to deal with."

Lupita nodded, but Sullivan wasn't sure she was entirely convinced. The train pulled into its next stop and she straightened up in her seat.

"I had my first job interview today," she said.

"That's terrific!"

Lupita shrugged.

"That is terrific, isn't it?" Sullivan asked.

"I graduated from university a few months ago. First class honours in sociology. Never been more proud of myself. The interview was in a clothes shop.

"I'm not saying that job isn't important. It is. But…I just thought I'd be doing something else. You work hard, go to school, study and get top grades, and then you get a job that you love. That's what my mum said. What all my teachers and family said."

Sullivan nodded. The world wasn't the same place as the one in which he grew up. He didn't have an easy time and worked hard for his money, but it wasn't like now. The statistics on the news for unemployment and young people were unfathomable.

"I can't get a job in my field. There just aren't any."

"Wait, you've been on this train longer than me. Aren't there any jobs nearer to you?"

"I've been signing on at the Job Centre for Jobseeker's Allowance. If I want to keep getting paid, I have to go to every interview they give me within a ninety-minute radius from my house."

"*Ninety minutes?*"

"Yeah. So I went to the interview today and I tried my best. But this isn't the life I want. Maybe that makes me entitled. I don't know. I keep getting rejected from jobs now for being overqualified. I thought all that time at university I was working towards something and now it feels like getting my degree did more harm than good."

She turned away from Sullivan and sniffled, but he could see in her reflection on the glass that her eyes were squeezed shut. He waited until they were open.

"I don't believe that," he said, softly.

"Why not?"

"Oh, there's this proverb – let me see if I remember it correctly. It's very old. Ancient, even – ah yes! I recall. I believe the saying goes, *life is a bitch.*"

Lupita snorted with surprise and then grinned.

"There's that lovely smile. Well, it's true, my dear. Life is one hell of a bitch. But there are things we do to survive and things we do to *live*. Benefits, jobs, terrible commutes... that all comes down to surviving. You do what you have to in order to get by. Even when society has betrayed you, you must persevere. Why? Because *living* is something else entirely. Family, friends, children, pets, hobbies…all the joys of this world. They are nothing to do with money or with any kind of system. The world can't touch those things. You loved studying sociology, yes?"

"I did," Lupita said.

"Then the rest of the world be damned! Better to study what you love and enrich yourself with a passion than to focus solely on survival. Life is a bitch, dear. You may as well have a little fun where you can. It'll make you a better person."

"I wish my mum saw it that way. She thinks the two are one and the same."

"For some people, they are. And that's okay. You just have to make sure you've found your *own* balance. That's what's important."

Lupita smiled again and used her thumb to rub the last jagged flakes from her fingernail.

"Okay, so what about you? What things are you living for?" she asked.

Sullivan leaned back and pressed into the headrest on his seat. The sound of dirt scattering across the coffin lid earlier rang in his ears again like the last droplets of water being wrung out from the final cloud in the sky.

The funeral was about as nice as a funeral could be; there was a decent turnout, the church was good-looking and not too cold like a lot of them were, and the service was a hearty mixture of happy reminiscence and quiet longing. Sullivan declined the family's request to deliver the eulogy. There wasn't anything he could say.

"Sullivan?" Lupita prompted.

"I was just at a funeral."

"Oh, I'm so sorry –"

"No, it's okay. Once you reach a certain age they come quite often. You get used to it. Feels like I'm going to a different funeral every week. It's more time-consuming than anything. At this rate, I'll be so busy going to other people's that I won't have time for my own!"

She smiled. Sullivan pulled the bag of chocolate eclairs out of his pocket and took one, before offering the bag to Lupita. They ate their sweets in silence.

"Whose was it?" she asked when her eclair was gone.

"My friend. Heath Jones," he said. Instead of replying, Lupita stared at him expectantly, so he continued, "there was nobody like Jonesy, I can tell you that much. Always up for an adventure and ready to laugh, but he wasn't daft. One of the best people I've ever known."

"How did you meet?"

"My wife, Darleen. She pushed me in the deep end at a party and Jonesy was the first person I talked to. Strange how one conversation can be life-changing. Naturally, you never know which ones will turn out that way, but that's part of the fun, eh?"

He thought back to the night he met Jonesy. Bad jazz was coming from a record player in the corner. It was the kind of jazz people who didn't listen to that genre put on when they wanted to pretend that they did. Tinsel was taped to the backs of chairs and sequins were scattered on tables. A buffet was at the back of the room. Everyone was in suits and dresses, holding glasses of Babycham.

"What do you call a chicken in a shell suit?" Jonesy asked.

"I don't know…"

"An *egg*."

"That's…uhh…that's not funny."

"Of course it's not funny! Have you ever heard something so shit?"

Jonesy stamped his foot when he laughed and reached into the back pocket of his trousers to fetch a cigar box. "Come with me, new fella," he said.

He led Sullivan out the rear exit into the courtyard. As Sullivan followed him, he looked back over his shoulder and shrugged to Darleen, who waved as she bit into a mini sausage roll.

The courtyard was bright despite it being half past eight on a December evening. There were several inches of undisturbed snow on what Sullivan assumed was the lawn. Moonlight caught the white ground and made it glister. Without a trace of wind in the air, the courtyard looked more like a still photograph than part of the world. Sullivan felt a twinge of guilt for their presence interfering with the picturesque scene. Jonesy didn't notice, stepping forward and scuffing the snow with the tip of his shoe that hung over the lip of the paving. He opened his small cigar box and pulled out some matches and two cigars.

"One for me and one for you, new fella," he said.

Sullivan took the cigar and waited for Jonesy to strike the match, holding the flame out to him first and then using it for himself before dropping it into the snow. He stuffed the box back into his pocket.

"What's your name?" Jonesy asked.

"Sullivan Protest. Yours?"

"Heath Jones. Jonesy, if you like. So you're the new town planner Jack hired, eh?"

Sullivan nodded. Jonesy chuckled and the vapour from his breath got caught in the cold air, mingling with the bitter

25

cigar smoke. "Well, Jack isn't too bad. Grumpy sod, but a good fella. You got family?" Jonesy said.

"My wife, Darleen. She's here tonight too."

Sullivan craned his neck and saw Darleen through the window chatting to a couple of other women. He pointed to her and Jonesy smiled.

"Ah yes, beautiful. You two have kids?"

"Not yet," Sullivan laughed, nervously.

"There's plenty of time for that yet. Best to get settled first, isn't it? Get a good house and job sorted out. Reckon that's what you've done here, right? It was the same for me and my Anna. We're expecting our first kiddo in May. Doc says it's a boy and gave us a picture of him. Poor sod looked like a peanut in his first photo. That's what I've been calling him, to Anna's chagrin. Trying to pick out a name though, that's the damndest thing, wouldn't you say? I like Sean, but Anna likes William. Might have to bite the bullet and flip a coin."

Jonesy carried on talking until their cigars were nothing more than stubs. Sullivan was happy to let him continue uninterrupted. It seemed a fast track to making a friend like Darleen wanted, but the more Jonesy talked, the more he began to genuinely like him.

"You're a good fella, Sully – can I call you Sully? Oh yes, a good fella for sure. I can tell. Why don't you and Darleen come for Sunday dinner next week?"

"Anna won't mind?"

"Not at all! You two would be most welcome. 'Tis the season and all that too. Here, take this." He pulled out his wallet and opened it to retrieve a business card. "Give us a ring sometime during the day tomorrow and we'll arrange it. Oh, best not called before 11am. I'm planning on knocking back a couple of whiskies tonight."

"Alright. Thank you."

"No need! Now, let's get back inside. It's bloody freezing."

"It's bloody freezing," Lupita said, pulling her jacket tighter around her.

"Pardon?" Sullivan said as the train slowed down to another stop.

"Is it just me or did this carriage get colder?"

Sullivan sat up and felt his toes press into his wet sock. His feet certainly could use some warming up. Maybe the temperature did drop. How long had he been thinking? Lupita looked at him with a furrowed brow before shrugging her shoulders and looking away.

"Sorry," he said. "Sometimes I feel like my head is tied up in knots. I get tangled in memories and spend hours each day trying to unpick them. I never do."

Lupita stared at him for a second and then reached into her handbag. When she looked up, she was holding a bag of jelly sweets. She opened it and extended them to Sullivan.

"You keep eclairs and I keep jellies. You never know when you need something sugary," she said.

"You're very kind," Sullivan said as he accepted one, "listening to an old fart like me witter on like I have been."

"I'm enjoying it." She paused for a moment. "I think it can be easier to talk to strangers. They say not to, I know, but I guess there's some stuff you'd rather say to a person you don't know. You ease your minds and then go your separate ways. Sometimes, that's just what you need."

The train continued on down the beaten line as rain whipped against the windows. It was both very quiet and loud to an irritating degree. The thunder of the tracks beneath them, the slamming of metal on metal, the scraping of brakes, and the intercom announcing stops every five minutes soon faded into white noise. Sullivan could have done without any of those sounds being there, but once he got used to them they were hardly noticeable. It wasn't until he got off a train that he realised just how loud the carriage was really. Apart from that, Lupita and Sullivan appeared to be the only ones talking – actually talking, not just idle chit-chat – and that made him breathe a little heavier. In just under twenty minutes, Sullivan would begin the walk back to his house and he'd never see Lupita again.

Home wasn't much to brag about. It was a small bungalow on Fieldview Crescent – a street once named aptly for Blackwater Field that lined the backs of the houses on the Crescent. It was only a small stretch of green among the patchwork of roads in the town, but the residents on the Crescent loved having the breathing room between them and everyone else. Recently, it was bought up by some retired millionaire from Oxford and construction had begun on a gaudy, three story nightmare that would soon dwarf all the bungalows and cast a permanent shadow upon them. Being an ex-town planner, Sullivan petitioned furiously to stop the building from going ahead, but he was soon shouted down. He wasn't a millionaire.

Sullivan's house was in the middle of Fieldview Crescent and the only one painted yellow. It was Darleen's idea and her favourite colour. The garden was also her doing. In the front, honeysuckle lined the fence, pansies bloomed from window boxes, and daffodils sprouted in between more flowers Sullivan couldn't identify. The grass was trimmed to a respectable one and a half inches — not too long to be considered unruly, but long enough to make the lawn appear fuller. The path up to the front door was paved and routinely washed with a power hose. Morning glories hung in a basket above the doorbell.

The front door opened into the kitchen. When Sullivan and Darleen moved into this house, which was both their first and last home, they were surprised to find that they never stopped cleaning the kitchen. As soon as they did anything in that room, it would need tidying. It became a running joke in the Protest household: one child, two of them, three meals a day, four kitchen cleanings, five servings of fruit and veg. He didn't have to do it so often anymore, although he knew when he got home today he needed to throw out the packaging from the previous night's microwave meal, which was still on the draining board.

Sullivan kept the curtains in the front of the house open to stop his neighbour from across the road, Mrs Ward, from coming over to check on him. She did a couple of times after he left the curtains closed past 10am and he never wanted her to come by again. Mrs Ward meant well, but he was past the point of excusing annoying people with good intentions. Instead, he kept all the curtains at the back of the house closed permanently. Not only did he feel there was some small, silly triumph to be had over Mrs Ward, but he didn't want to see the monstrosity being constructed in what used to be Darleen's favourite picnic spot.

"Alright, Quinn, dish the sandwiches out," Darleen said to their son, now ten years old.

"Ham for Dad," Quinn said, handing out their lunch, "jam for me, and chicken for you, Mum."

29

They ate in silence. Blackbirds whistled from somewhere in the taller grass. Grasshoppers rattled in the heat. Bees stitched invisible patterns in the humid air. They scrunched up the empty bags from their food and shoved them into Darleen's satchel.

"Mum…" Quinn said after a few minutes, "why can't I have a brother to play with?"

"Not this again," Darleen said.

"But it would be so fun! I'd teach him everything I know like how to play football and how to make paper aeroplanes and how to tie his shoelaces and I wouldn't let him fall or hurt himself and I would look after him properly and I –"

"Enough, Quinn," Sullivan said.

Quinn pouted and stopped talking, the words 'it's not fair' visible on his lips to his parents, even though they went unspoken.

"Look, Quinnie," Darleen said, "it takes a lot to make a new baby. A long time and even some pain for Mummy. There's no guarantee it would even be a boy. You might end up with a sister. Your dad and I are happy with just you."

"I just…I think I'd make a good big brother," he said, quietly.

"Of course you would. You're the best boy in the whole world. But that's why we only need one of you, silly."

Quinn frowned and looked from his mother to his father. "How do babies get made?"

"Christ almighty," Darleen laughed. "You fancy taking this one, Dad?"

"Not on your nelly," Sullivan chuckled. "Come on, kid, get the football and we'll have a kick-about. Leave Mum alone for a bit."

That night in bed, Sullivan and Darleen talked about getting a puppy for Quinn. A few months later, Rabbit joined the family and they learned what happens when a ten-year-old is allowed free reign over naming duties.

*I must remember to call Quinn when I get in*, Sullivan thought to himself on the train. It had been a couple of weeks since they last spoke on the phone. Quinn was nearing fifty years old now, living in Suffolk with his wife and their three boys. He never became a big brother, but seemed to enjoy being a father much more.

"Could I –" Lupita began, but stopped short. "No, never mind."

"What is it?"

"It doesn't matter."

"Suit yourself, dear. Although it was you who said that sometimes it's easier to talk to strangers."

"Yes. I did say that," she paused. "Well, it's about my mum."

"Go on," Sullivan said.

Lupita stopped again and looked at Sullivan, but not in the way she'd looked at him before. This time it was directly into his eyes. "I think you're a good person," she said.

Sullivan thought about the last six months. About Mrs Ward. About not going to the funeral reception earlier. About not delivering Jonesy's eulogy. The packaging from last night's meal on the draining board. A fortnight without speaking to Quinn. Construction sites. Honeysuckle. Darleen.

"I don't know," he said.

"Maybe you're right. We just met thirty minutes ago. Or maybe I'm right and you can't see it," she smiled. Then, as if remembering what the conversation was really about, her face dropped. "I've never told anyone this before. Maybe there's some safety in strangers after all. I think my mum is sick."

*Sick.* A loaded word that could mean too many things. Hungover, fed up, a cold, the flu, terminal. All fit under the suffocating umbrella of *sick*.

"She's losing weight. Her appetite changed a little, but she's still eating plenty. Even so, pounds just fall off her and she seems more tired than usual. People have started complimenting her, you know. On losing weight. Like she's more beautiful or better off now she's thinner. That makes me angry. Seething. She's always been beautiful. And now I think she's ill, people are *praising* her.

"I can't get her to see a doctor. She refuses to go. She spends all day on her feet until she's near to fainting. Migraines have been hitting her too. And she's invited the whole family up to visit tomorrow, which will only give her more to do. I'm so angry with her, Sullivan, and that makes me mad at myself. What if she is sick? What if I'm wasting time by being upset with her? I don't know what to do."

Lupita began chipping off her nail polish again, this time not bothering to do it over the table, instead letting the flakes fall over her suit and get caught on her trousers. Sullivan's breath felt solid in his throat and he understood briefly what it felt like to be asphyxiated.

"I understand," he said, "that urge to want to do something and not be able to. It's okay to be angry. Life is a bitch, remember? But anger…anger is never genuine. It's a costume. A way of dressing up pain, fear, grief…none of us are ever really angry. Not ever. We only pretend to be because the alternative is too hard to face."

"I just want her to get help. See someone about it, just in case."

"Why?"

"What?"

"Why do you want her to get help, if she doesn't want it?" Sullivan asked.

"For her, so she can get better."

"My dear," he said, leaning in and being as gentle as he could, "if she doesn't want to speak to a doctor, there's nothing that can be done. You can't help someone who doesn't want to be helped."

Lupita nodded so slightly that only Sullivan next to her was able to make it out.

"I think I'm a good daughter," she whispered.

"I'm sure you are."

"All I've ever wanted is for my mum to see me live out my dreams. I think that's what she wants. For me to get a job, a house, a family...but all that stuff, the job interview today, that's not my dream. She's conflating money and domesticity with my success and she'll never see me happy like that."

Sullivan leaned back and scratched his chin, silently berating himself for getting involved before correcting his thoughts. Lupita clearly wanted to speak, but it was a long time since he spoke to someone so personally. It was like riding a bike. People say you never forget how to do it. An empath is always an empath. Lately, Sullivan wasn't so sure. These skills could dull, weaken, and even break altogether. Riding a bike was easily forgotten. Reaching out to others could be too.

"Take it from me," he said eventually, "as a father, what most parents want is to leave our kids behind with stability. Happiness and dreams come later. You find those things for yourself. But a strong foundation is what we can give you. I'll bet anything that's what she wants and I'll eat my brolly if I'm wrong."

"Do you think she knows?" Lupita asked and Sullivan knew from her tone that she wasn't enquiring about what he'd just said.

"I think if you've noticed her ailing, chances are she's known for longer than you."

"That's what I thought too. I just can't believe, after years of biting my head off for less, she's being so *careless*."

"I think, my dear, you need to figure out how you're really feeling, beneath the anger. Anger always puts its weight on someone else. Figure out what's really going on so you can carry your own emotions and lift them off the shoulders of your mum. She has autonomy here, however much you might hate the way she's handling it."

"Do you think I'm making it worse? Or maybe I'm just imagining it. I don't know reality from my own mind half the time."

"If you say it's happening, then I believe you."

Lupita nodded again slowly.

"I'm pretty certain about this," she said. "I have a feeling. An intuition. I know her. I *know* her. And she's changing."

She reached down to her handbag again and pulled out her purse, knocking a box of mints as she did. They sounded like a bottle of pills rattling.

"Get those bloody things away from me," Darleen said.

"Here, this is my mum," Lupita said, pulling out a photograph of a middle-aged woman in a fuchsia sari.

Sullivan stared at the mints and then rubbed his eyes. He took the photograph from Lupita and felt warmed by the huge smile radiating from the face in the image.

"Her name is Chandhni."

"How lovely. She looks very happy," Sullivan said.

"She does," she said, stroking her mother's cheek with a finger before putting the photo away.

She nudged the mints again as she dropped her purse back into her bag.

"I told you, Sully, I've had enough of those evil little capsules. Just let me rest," Darleen said.

Sullivan bit the inside of his cheek.

"It must be wonderful to grow up with different cultures," he said, trying to talk over the beeping of doors opening and closing as people got off the train at the current stop.

"Oh for God's sake, do we need to have all these blasted machines? They make more fuss than they're worth," Darleen said.

"It can be," Lupita said, "though it's not always easy."

"I don't suppose it is," Sullivan said, wringing his hands together.

"I love my mum. Sometimes I wish she'd do things differently. But I do love her. I just think…I think if she saw a doctor and it was bad, she could get a diagnosis or a time estimate. Something to make it all less of a shock, if she…" Lupita trailed off.

"It's always a shock," Sullivan said. "Even when you know it's coming, it's still abrupt. When it happens, it always hits you out of nowhere."

All the colour drained from Sullivan's world in the doctor's office. He squeezed Darleen's hand as though if he let go she'd float away out the open window like a balloon. Only occasional words pricked his ears. *Tumour. Malignant. Sorry.* Everything else faded into the cacophony of the world outside: cars revving, birds squalling, and babies crying. On the drive home, he didn't realise the radio was on until Darleen leaned over and switched it off.

A few months later, she spent some time in the hospital surrounded by whirring machines, but it made them overly conscious of the truth. Eventually, he brought her home. In these last few days, they could lie to themselves.

Sullivan tried to make her as comfortable as he could. She was on bed rest permanently now. He went out and bought new pillows – the most expensive, fluffy ones he could find – and bright yellow cases for them. There was always a tub of raspberry ice cream in the freezer. The windowsill was cluttered with vases full of flowers from the garden. He painted her nails for her and they giggled madly at how terrible he was at it.

"Thank god you're not doing my make-up too. You'll have me looking like a bloody Picasso painting!" she laughed.

At night, they slept next to each other holding hands and every morning that she woke up, Sullivan sang while he made breakfast. Long gone were the days of cereal and toast. It would be pancakes, omelettes, and the dirtiest, greasiest fry-ups known to man. Sometimes she could only manage a little, but other days she finished her plate before Sullivan.

"Careful, darling," he'd joke, "you're starting to eat like a Labrador too!"

She snorted and elbowed him gently.

People came to visit. Jonesy showed up with his wife, Anna, bearing chocolates and a bouquet of pink lilies to add to the burgeoning garden in their bedroom window. Quinn and his family came down in separate cars, so his wife could take the boys back after a couple of days and Quinn could stay behind. One afternoon, Darleen was feeling particularly tired and decided to nap, so Sullivan and Quinn made a couple of coffees and took them to drink outside in the back yard, which wasn't as pleasant as the front garden, but it was away from the prying eyes of Mrs Ward.

"You didn't have to hang back. You know, if you wanted to go home with the boys," Sullivan said.

"I did have to, Dad," Quinn said.

They sipped their coffees, staring over the fence at Blackwater Field, just recently sold.

"What I wouldn't give to have a place like that to take my kids for picnics," Quinn said.

"We were unbelievably lucky."

"We were," Quinn paused. "Dad? Do you ever feel guilty?"

"What for?"

"With Mum. Sometimes it feels like she's the one helping us cope. Like she's being strong for us."

"I know what you mean. But it's not like her to do anything else. She's always the one in charge. The one taking care of things."

Quinn tapped his nails against his mug and stared down at his feet.

"I worry about you, Dad," he said, quietly.

"What on earth for?"

"That you'll be lonely."

Sullivan breathed in sharply and shut his eyes. Then he put his arm around his son, who was both almost fifty and five years old simultaneously in Sullivan's head, and pulled him closer.

"Now, you listen to me, kid. I'm going to be just fine. A lifetime with a family like I've had is enough to see me through. So don't you fret about your old man."

Quinn leaned into his father for the first time in decades and the pair of them sat, huddled together on the cold, hard steps outside the back door. As they finished their coffees,

Sullivan's eyes settled on the rock next to the lilac tree on the far end of the yard, where they buried Rabbit countless years ago.

"He was a good dog," Quinn said, who must have followed Sullivan's eye line.

"The best. Shame about his name though."

"Hey! I was ten."

"Still…*Rabbit?* He was a great, thumpin' German Shepard! I don't think you could have given him a wetter name, short of Bunny."

"Bunny? See, I have been considering getting my boys a puppy…*Bunny* does have an awfully good ring to it, now that you say it out loud…"

"Oh, don't you dare!" Sullivan chuckled.

Quinn got up and grabbed the mugs in one hand, extending his other to his dad to help him stand.

"Come on, better get the washing up done before Mum wakes. Then we'll only have one kitchen cleaning left before bed," Quinn said.

"Oh, joy."

That night, Darleen fell asleep against Sullivan's chest. He kissed the top of her head and nodded off. In the morning, only one of them woke.

"What do you mean, 'it's always a shock?'" Lupita asked.

"My wife. She died. About six months ago."

"Oh, Sullivan, I'm so sorry."

"It's okay. We – my son and I – knew it was coming. She had cancer. We caught it too late. You always know that at some point your loved ones will die, but nothing makes it more real than that. You spend every waking minute anticipating, but when it finally happens, you can't believe it.

"She was in the hospital for a while getting treatment, but it was hell for her. Had her up all hours of the night vomiting…terrible pains and exhaustion…in the end, we just brought her home. She stopped taking her pills. She wanted to be normal before…"

Sullivan's voice ran out of sound. His lips kept moving, but he couldn't finish the sentence. Lupita laid a hand on his shoulder.

"I see what you mean. About my mum," she said.

"Yes. If I had it my way, she'd have been in that damn hospital until her last breath, and I'd have made her miserable for it. Sometimes, it's not up to us."

"Was she…was she happier? Being left to it?"

"I hope so," Sullivan said. "The last thing she ever did was smile. We were married fifty years and I swear I can remember every single time she smiled."

She wasn't smiling in her coffin. Her face was resting as though she had only shut her eyes for a moment, but would be up and about in no time. Sullivan rested his hands on the edge and stared at his wife.

Darleen would have made such a fuss if she knew he was burying her in the blue dress he gave her, eons ago now. She'd tell him off because it was a dusty old thing even though the style was too youthful. There was a small pink stain from Quinn's ancient raspberry ice cream near the hem.

"She'd hate that," Quinn said, coming up behind his father.

"Wouldn't she just," Sullivan agreed.

"Can almost hear her screaming down at us."

They smiled. Sullivan looked over to his son, whose eyes were struggling to see through the tears that glazed across them. He let go of the coffin and put his arm around his boy.

"Well, she'll just have to wait a while before she can kick off at us, won't she? In the mean-time, you start thinking of excuses to save your old man from an eternity of her wrath, eh?" Sullivan joked, wiping his eyes.

Lupita was prodding Sullivan's arm. He shook his head, coming out of a trance. She was trying to pass him a tissue.

"What?" he said.

"For your eyes."

Sullivan nodded and accepted the tissue, not sure when exactly he began to cry and feeling abysmally guilty that poor Lupita had to put up with a snivelling stranger on her journey home.

"I'm sorry," he said.

"Don't be," she smiled, softly.

Lupita's phone rang for the third time during Sullivan's stint on the train. She looked at the screen, drew in her breath, and answered.

"Hi, Mum," she said, "I'm nearly there…okay…yeah, sure…definitely…alright, well I'll see you in about half an hour…okay…I love you."

As she put her phone back, the intercom announced that they would shortly be arriving at Sullivan's stop. Forty-five minutes of his life had flashed away before his eyes, but he considered them well spent. He had Jonesy to thank for it. Saying that about anyone else would be crude, but with Jonesy it was exactly what he could expect.

"Spent the afternoon chatting to a young lass on the train, eh? I'm glad one of us got something good from my funeral. You're welcome, fella," Sullivan could hear him say, followed by that great booming laugh of his.

"Right, well, this is me," he said, patting his pockets

to make sure he had everything and stashing *To Kill a Mockingbird* safely in his jacket. He would try to read more before bed.

"Hang on," Lupita said, retrieving the sweets from her bag and offering another to Sullivan. "One for the road?"

"Thank you."

The train began to slow as they encroached on the final mile before the stop.

"I guess I'll see you never," she said.

"Never," he agreed, smiling.

"It was nice talking to you, Sullivan. Take care."

"You too, Lupita."

Sullivan took one last look at her in her navy suit, lilac blouse, thick black plait, and disastrously chipped pink nails. Then he nodded, popped the jelly into his mouth, stood up, and made his way towards the doors.

He decided to stand on the platform and watch her go. Lupita grinned when she saw him and they waved to each other. Pulling his umbrella out of his carrier bag, he opened it up and waited for the train to move. He made an internal promise that as soon as he got home he would throw away the rubbish on the draining board and call Quinn. They had so much to catch up on. Then the train started up and Lupita sped away from him down the tracks and out of his life. That was the sad thing about friendships. They weren't all made to last forever, including the good ones. Some people are only supposed to know each other for a small amount of time. Perhaps even the length of a single train journey.

**LEANDER**Huckaby's face mashed further into the palm of his hand as his eyelids drooped, lulled to sleep by the wisps of hair that fluttered free from Ms Bochart's ponytail. All he had to do was survive ten more minutes of Science and he was home-free. As he became aware he was falling asleep, his head snapped up and he snorted. Ms Bochart's steely stare fell heavy on his head like an axe on a chopping block.

"I trust you slept well, Leander," she rasped.

Mumbling an apology, Leander tried to refocus his attention on the class. Next to him, Trisha Yellowwood popped pink bubbles under her breath from some forbidden bubble-gum. It was against the rules to chew gum, but she did so often that it was almost an accessory to her school uniform. Leander stole a glance at her and half-wondered if she might be pretty, but shivered the thought away. Trisha was a *girl*.

"Your homework for next week is on trees. We'll be looking at summer branch drop," Ms Bochart said. "Sometimes in the summer, older branches will break off trees, but the cause for this is still unknown. They just fall away with no obvious explanation."

When the last bell of the day rang, Leander began the long walk home. It was down past Willoughby Way where Robbie Bakerfield picked him up by the ankles and shook pennies from his pockets. It was beyond the old stone steps down to the canal. Sycamore trees grew over the pathway, buckling under the weight of their seeds that spun in the wind like helicopters. Did these trees lose their branches when they were old? His house was even further than Conkers Creek, a secret spot behind the houses on Oak Avenue where he knew his brother took girls to *kiss*. Leander thought of Trisha Yellowwood again and her pout that glazed her gum with saliva as bubbles pushed through her wet lips. Who would kiss *that*?

Leander's street – Poppy Drive – was different to the surrounding rows. First of all, it wasn't a street at all, but rather a large alleyway between Maple Road and Blossom Street. It wasn't paved, so it was subjected to new dips and bumps after each rainfall. Only four houses lined Poppy Drive – two on the left side and two on the right – and each was responsible for maintaining the section of road outside their property. The second reason Leander's street was different to the others was that it was where Citroen Sid lived. As Leander rounded the corner onto his driveway, he saw Sid at his usual 3:45pm antics.

Sid was lying in the middle of the road face down, panting. With each exhalation, dirt from the ground blew up in clouds. Leander thought about whether Sid sucked any into his mouth when he breathed in. He was eyeing up the rocks along his section of the driveway. He moved them exactly half a centimetre forward every morning, slowly expanding the boundary of his land five millimetres at a time. Abruptly pushing himself to his feet and saying a word Leander knew not to repeat, Sid brushed himself off and noticed Leander staring at him.

"You tell your [CENSORED] mum to stay off my mother[CENSORED] property," he snapped.

Leander's eyes widened. He watched Sid go into his house and slam the door. It wasn't the first time he'd heard that word, but normally when somebody said it around him they immediately looked at the ground and apologised. Nobody had ever, *ever* said it so proudly. Leander decided that he liked the word. It sounded strong and grown up which, so his father told him, was exactly why he couldn't say it. He wasn't old enough to swear yet. At what point then, he wondered, would he be old enough to say…[CENSORED]? Going inside, Leander dumped his bag on the kitchen counter.

"No, no, no. Not *there*. Put it over *there*," his mother said, gesturing that his bag belonged on a hook with the coats and not, in fact, in the way of everything.

She was kneading dough on a pastry board. White flour speckled the curls in her hair. Unruly butter slid up her fingers. Their dog Rosco sat at her feet hoping that, in her clumsiness, she would drop the pastry altogether.

"Mum," Leander said, helping himself to some apple juice from the fridge, "Citroen Sid said you need to stop meddling."

"For the last time, stop calling him that. He's just Sid."

"Mum, Just Sid said you need to stop meddling."

"You know what I meant."

She began pushing a rolling pin over the dough before pulling out a ruler and making nicks in it with a knife.

"Why you doing that for?" Leander asked.

"Why *are* you doing that? Speak properly."

"Okay, why *are* you doing that?"

"To make sure it's the right size for the casserole dish."

"What did Cit – *Sid* – mean by meddling?"

"I was moving those blummin' rocks back."

"Why?"

"Because the further out he puts them, the closer people drive to our property."

"So?"

"So I don't want the road moved right by us, with traffic smashing into our hedges and leaving potholes along our driveway. I want the road where it is."

"Why don't you tell on him?"

"I tried," she said, placing the dough into the dish and folding the edges up. "I told the Reeves next door, but they went on again about how Sid's been here forty years. They don't care. Bloody useless." She threw the pastry trimmings in the bin and Rosco began to whine. "Take the dog for a walk, Lee."

"But, muuuuum!"

"Take him. You both need some fresh air and he's driving me barmy."

"I just had a walk! I walked home from school!"

"Two won't kill you."

Leander sighed and grabbed the leash, snapping it to Rosco's collar. He took his keys from the front pocket of his schoolbag, put the backpack on its correct hook in the proper place, and went back outside.

It was obvious to everyone that Sid earned his nickname from the dozen Citroen cars that littered his yard. They were his prized possessions, but he didn't treat them like they were important. Instead, they rotted and fell apart in the overgrown grass. Their metal corpses filled with rust. Weeds tangled themselves in the tyres. Birds flew through smashed windows to peck stuffing from the seats. Every now and then, Sid would acquire another car for his graveyard at an auction, dump it with the others, and never look at it again. Rumours about this odd behaviour went around the school. Some said that Sid bought a Citroen every time he murdered someone and the bodies were buried in the yard under the cars. Leander shuddered as he walked past them. He doubted this was true, but even murderers have to live somewhere, right?

At least his mother refused to put up with Sid. Every morning she'd take Rosco for a walk before she went to work and on the way back home she'd kick all the rocks into the hedges. Then Sid would come out at 7:45am and put them all back a little closer to Leander's house, measuring the distance as accurately as he could after they had all been booted out of place.

"If he took care of those cars like he does with those blasted rocks, his yard wouldn't be such a tip," Leander's mother said.

The walk with Rosco went quickly. Leander didn't hate walking the dog, he'd just rather be doing something else like watching his favourite cartoon, *Marco and Rodney*, a show about two space cowboys who went on intergalactic adventures. It was definitely for grown-ups, because they used some pretty bad language like what Sid said earlier. Leander's parents didn't know. They just figured it was a cartoon, so it was appropriate for him to watch. As long as Leander used his headphones, his mum and dad were none the wiser.

When Leander walked past Citroen Sid's house coming home, he noticed something strange. The front door was open, but Sid wasn't anywhere to be seen. The detail that made it weird was the *type* of open the door was; it wasn't cracked or ajar. It was all the way open. In the years Leander had been living on Poppy Drive, Sid never left the door open. Overpowered by curiosity, Leander tightened his grip on Rosco's leash and crept a little closer to Sid's house. He could see right through the living room in the front to the kitchen in the back. There was no movement, only the flickering of Citroen Sid's kitchen light and his cemetery of cars. Leander gulped.

Sneaking closer – treading the ground underneath him from the back of his heel to the tip of his toe – Leander craned his neck to see more. Still there was no one. The carpet in the living room was thick and dark. It looked brown – though it could have been red – but it was hard to tell as all the curtains were pulled shut. The sofa was against the far wall, but all its cushions were on the floor by a tall, ominous bookcase. Nothing matched. Leander tied Rosco to the fence post and drew in a deep breath. It didn't look like Sid was home. If he went inside, he'd be known at school as the boy who went into Citroen Sid's house. He'd have the inside scoop. He might even be popular. Maybe Robbie Bakerfield would stop stealing his pocket money and want to be friends instead. The compulsion to go inside became too strong. As Marco and Rodney would say in their cartoon, *buckle up and [CENSORED] it.*

Leander stood in Citroen Sid's doorway, his eyes adjusting to his surroundings. As he stepped inside, he was immediately hit with a smell he couldn't identify. It was like old bananas, but burned; similar to custard, but with a sour note. It resembled the warm milk that Leander liked before bed, but if it was microwaved in a plastic cup that melted a little into the milk. Leander had no idea where it was coming from, but the whole house reeked of it.

Everything was covered in dust and it was clear that nothing had been disturbed in years. In the corner, there was a big square radio with huge black CDs. Leander had never seen anything like it. He sat down cross-legged in front of a large box full of the CDs and began to flick through them. As the first one fell forward, it shot dust out into his face and Leander coughed. Pulling his school shirt up over his nose, he browsed the rest of them. They were all names he'd never heard before: *Fats Domino, Ella Fitzgerald, Duke Ellington…* They looked old anyway and, as Leander's schoolmates made him blatantly aware, nothing old was good. New was undoubtedly always better. Maybe that's why trees dropped their old branches; they were just making room for better ones.

Suddenly, the door behind him closed. Leander shot up off the floor. He spun around. Citroen Sid towered above him, palm spread flat against the front door.

"A visitor," Sid said.

Leander needed to explain that he came in because the door was open and wanted to check on him, but as he went to speak it occurred to him how stupid that would sound. Not only was it a lie, but an open door wasn't an invitation and Leander knew it. Instead, he kept his mouth shut and stared at his mysterious neighbour.

"I didn't know you were comin' today. Please, sit…" Sid went to gesture to the sofa, but saw that all the cushions were on the floor. "How did they get there? Have you been makin' a mess again?"

Leander wondered what Sid meant by 'again' as he watched him put the cushions back.

"How about a cuppa, eh?" Sid said, smiling. His hands shook as he beckoned to Leander. "Why don't you help me?"

Cautiously, Leander followed him into the kitchen. Sid flicked the kettle on and took two cups down from a cupboard.

"I wondered when you were comin' over. You always say 'soon' on the phone, but it feels like forever," Sid said.

"I-I've never phoned you."

"Then what was last night all about?"

"What?"

"Don't be stupid," Sid snapped, slamming his hand on the counter and making Leander jump. "Has your mother put you up to this? Plannin' some joke on me?"

"My mum?"

"Just because she has custody don't mean I'm some extra in your life!" Sid shouted.

Leander began to tremble. Nothing Sid was saying made any sense and he got angry so quickly. *Does he know who I am?* he thought. *How could a person forget someone they see every day?* The boiling water shook the kettle violently before it finished. Sid drew in several deep breaths and then smiled at Leander.

"I haven't seen you in so long. But I have a surprise for you."

"A surprise?"

"Yeah. Remember that car you said you loved? That nice Citroen we saw at the fair a couple of weeks back?"

"C-Citroen?"

"I know you're far too young, but I bought one. Thought maybe you'd enjoy going for drives with me in it until we can get you your own one day."

"You bought a Citroen for me?"

"Of course. You're my boy."

Leander's mouth was dry. He heard a faint bark and remembered that Rosco was still tied up outside. Sid put the cups back into the cupboard without making any tea and Leander glanced over at the front door, trying to visualise the distance between this kitchen and his own.

"Can I go have a look at it?" Leander said.

"Sure, and then we can go for a drive."

"G-great! It's cold out; you should get your coat. I'll meet you outside."

They smiled at each other and then Leander tried to walk outside as normally as possible. Once he was out Sid's door, he ran to Rosco who leapt up when he saw him. Leander grabbed his leash and fumbled with the knot. Finally, he wrenched Rosco free and they ran back home together. He shut the door so hard that the ceiling light shook and then he bolted it. He lowered the blinds in the window. Dragging Rosco into the kitchen and throwing his bag on the counter, he was barely able to catch his breath.

"Hey, hey!" His mother began to chastise him for leaving his bag in the way again, before noticing that something was wrong. "Leander? Are you okay?"

Leander shook his head.

"What happened?"

"I was at Sid's."

"*Sid's*? Why the bloody hell were you at Sid's?"

"His door was open."

"So you just walked in? Leander Huckaby, do you have any idea how irresponsible that is? Not only could you have been in danger, but it was extremely..."

Leander could hear her telling him off, but he wasn't listening. He tuned her voice out, nodding at the right times and keeping his gaze low, trying to look ashamed.

Later, he sat on the sofa with his mum watching the television. Rosco lay across Leander's feet so he could feel the dog's warm belly move with each breath over his toes. It was hard to focus on the programme. Whatever it was, it lacked the snap and spirit of *Marco and Rodney*, and nobody at all said [CENSORED]. Besides, his thoughts were still with Sid. Leander turned his attention to the window next to him, looking across the street to Sid's house. The moon highlighted the tops of the rocks with which Sid lined his stretch of Poppy Drive and glinted across the sloping roof. Everything else was cradled in the soft black of the quiet night.

"Lee…" his mum said, coaxing him back into the room. "I'm sorry for getting so cross earlier. I was worried."

Leander nodded and watched her face. Her lips were small and puckered, pulling a few extra shadows across her skin by the orange glow of the table lamp. Rosco sighed deeply the way dogs do when they're just about to drift off to sleep. Leander felt Rosco's heartbeat drumming along the bones in his foot. He pictured his feet like the inside of a piano; Rosco's pulse was the hammer that hit the strings, but in this empty evening neither one of them made a noise.

"Sid isn't very well," she said eventually.

"He's sick?"

"Sort of. But it's not his body. It's his brain. He doesn't remember things very well."

"He needs a doctor."

"He has one, Lee. But even doctors can't fix everything."

"Can we help him?"

He felt her hand brush the back of his. For a moment, Leander saw her glance out the window. Then she tugged her feet out from underneath Rosco's bottom and stuck them into the pair of slippers she'd left by the end table.

"No. We can't help him," she said, picking up the remote and turning off the television.

"So what do we do?"

"We carry on as normal, Lee. Now get to bed; you've got school in the morning."

He kissed the top of Rosco's head the way he did every night and stole one last look at Sid's house. An overwhelming heaviness rose in his chest, but Leander couldn't define it. Somehow his world felt different tonight. There wasn't any medicine to fix Sid, his Citroens decaying with his memory as he waited for a day that would never come. What if Leander's brain caught a cold like Sid's and he couldn't remember anything? Maybe Sid was like a piano too and something else was playing on him. It certainly felt like it and that, Leander decided, was truly...*fucked*.

# THESE ARMS

**THEY** were forget-me-nots. She knew that from sitting on her father's lap as a young girl and reading those outdoor magazines together that he loved.

"Pretty," she said.

"Just like you, princess."

"Blue."

"Just like me."

Six decades on, the faintest smile flickered in Joan's eyes as she stroked the tiny petals between her fingers and thought about pulling them up. They were weeds after all. Was it enough to let something live just for being beautiful?

"They're called forget-me-nots," he once said, pulling her against his chest.

"Why?"

"Whenever you see them, it means a person who isn't around anymore is telling you how much they love you."

"From Heaven?"

"Sure, princess."

Joan let the flowers go. They could stay a little longer.

It was a hot day for Anglesey. The end of summer hovered above the island as a thick, invisible dome. As Joan peeled off her gardening gloves, she noticed how clammy her palms were and how her fingers slipped past each other, barely touching. Her father used to knit his huge hands into hers and spin her round, dancing in the living room together with his favourite song on the record player.

*"These arms of miiiiiiiiine,"* he crooned, swirling her around and pulling Joan into a hug that completely enveloped her.

The gloves fell from Joan's hands onto the lawn. She didn't pick them up, only stepped around them on her way back into the house. Inside, Ffiona was standing at the kitchen sink, filling the kettle with water.

"Fancy a panad?" she asked.

"Sure, ta."

Joan watched her daughter fix two cups of tea in silence. The kettle rumbled away in the corner, steaming and adding to the sweltering humidity in the room. Ffiona's yellow dress swished against her calves. A blackbird's song came in through the open window, over the low hum of the boiling water. Joan wiped her eyes on her shirt sleeve before Ffiona turned back around.

"Here you go, mam," she said, handing Joan's drink to her. "Shall we sit outside?"

"Good idea," Joan replied, following Ffiona into the garden across from where she just was, to the table and chairs underneath the rowan tree.

"Lovely day."

"Too bloody hot for me."

"I know, mam, but in winter it's too bloody cold, in spring it's too bloody wet, and in autumn it's too bloody mercurial," Ffiona laughed. "I'll take the heat any day."

"You weren't made for this climate. You must have been Spanish or Italian in another life."

"You always say that, mam."

"Consistency is key," Joan said, taking a sip from her mug. "Much like this. You always make a good cuppa."

A brief breeze tangled itself in the branches of the tree and a few red berries dropped down onto the grass around them.

They sat in silence. Joan's eyes drifted along the flowerbed to her gloves. If it rained they would be ruined. It didn't matter.

"*These arms of miiiiiiiiine, they are lonely, lonely and feeling bluuuuue,*" her father sang, lifting Joan up onto his feet so that when he moved she was in time with him.

"Daddy!" she shrieked and they giggled together.

"Mam?" Ffiona said, pulling Joan back to the garden. "Are you okay?"

"Aye, sorry. I was just thinking."

"About?"

"I have some forget-me-nots blooming over there. You see them? The little blue ones sprawling about between the pansies."

"I see them."

Ffiona frowned. Joan hated when she crumpled her face up in that sad, confused way. A blackbird swooped down and courageously ventured over to nibble at the fallen berries. Was this the same one who was singing before? It was unlikely. There were so many of them and they were all the same. It was always that song too. Joan could barely stand to be in the garden anymore.

She moved into this house when her husband left her a couple of years ago. She never knew rage like she did that day. In the evening, Ffiona came over. Even then, Joan felt awful that Ffiona decided to see her and not Gordon. It was a stupid thing to feel guilty over, but this was never the life she wanted to give her daughter. There was supposed to be a sense of security that settled in with being married for forty years. Where was the stability? The eternity?

Ffiona was kind enough to turn up with a bottle of Merlot.

Joan stared down at her red reflection floating in the top of her wine. This wasn't her body. When she pictured herself in her mind, she never looked the way she did now. She imagined herself with her *then*-body – the softness of her wedding night with those peaks and valleys she could share with the blissful denial of mortality. She thought of how Gordon had loved her, brokered the give and take of their tide that night. But forty years came like a current and drowned them. Who was she now?

She could torch the house down, and why the fuck shouldn't she? After all, it was only her left. Ffiona encouraged her to move.

"Mam, you know a lovely place by the beach would suit you better. Sunshine, waves, the salt air...it would be ace," Ffiona said, as if Joan wanted to be another old biddy by the sea.

She supposed to herself that she'd need a new home if she set this one alight. The thought of erasing all evidence of their marriage – and Gordon's betrayal – in a blaze changed her mind. Maybe she could do something else. Breast implants were a thing women got, right? She could get a perfect pair of new tits shoved into this stranger's body. Or perhaps she could take an extended holiday and fuck off to Bali like Julia Roberts did in that film once...what was it called? She could burn *Gordon's* house down AND fuck off to Bali. With new tits. And a hunk called Pedro.

"Mam?" Ffiona said. "Are you listening?"

"Sorry. Yes. I'll think about it."

Ffiona raised her eyebrows and pulled out a powder compact, staring into the mirror on the inside of the lid, primping and pouting. Joan looked at her own reflection again before throwing the rest of the drink down her throat and swallowing hard. While she poured another glass she fantasised about what Pedro might look like and how exactly she would go about meeting someone like him. If Gordon could start again at his age, surely Joan could too. But she already knew it wasn't the same. The compact snapped shut as Ffiona sighed and reached her hand across to Joan's knee.

"You need to take care of yourself, mam. You know I'm always here for you, of course, but you need to be here for yourself most of all."

She nodded and drank. When Ffiona left and she was alone again, Joan drew a bath. There were two bath bombs left over from the Christmas present Ffiona gave her. Once was elderflower and jasmine. The other was spiced apple. Joan stared at them – one in each hand – turning them over. Was elderflower or apple better for a soon-to-be divorcée to marinate in? Screw it, Joan thought, and flung them into the water together. Let them both go.

After a couple of weeks, the anger drained away into grief, and then the distant echoes of sadness. Soon it was only a small cry, reverberating in her bones. If she tuned into it, tears would come almost immediately. Instead, Joan ignored it, continuing her days aware that it was there, but no longer acknowledging it. That was hard to do now. It was only in the understanding that Joan would never see him again that she felt strong enough to let him into her thoughts.

"We haven't talked about it," Ffiona said, following her mother's mind effortlessly as they sat together in the garden.

"No."

"Should we?"

"We could. If it would help you."

"And what about you? Would it help *you*?"

"I'm not sure."

Ffiona nodded and lowered her head. The look of a child who wanted something they couldn't have never faded as the years shaped them. It was a universal expression.

"Look, Fee, I've not been sure about your dad in a long time. He did that. Planted the uncertainty in my heart. In this family. But this is…this is something else. I don't know how to live without my hurt. How can I let it go to feel another?"

"This isn't about you, mam," Ffiona said gently. "I'm sorry. You know I value your pain. Even though I loved dad so much, I will always share that sadness with you. But there is room in a heart for more than one crack."

"*Lonely and feeling bluuuuue…*" her father span around inside her head.

Joan always remembered her dad fondly, even when he was gruff or reserved. Eventually, distance became intrinsic to his entire existence and that searching look in his eyes was constant. Throughout her life, she never came close to understanding where he went when nobody was looking. Every day was a funeral for him, a procession and a speech, the long walk between graves until he arrived at the one he wanted, and said goodbye. Life was only a condition to him; a state to wait out until he got what he truly desired.

Losing her mother was worse for him. She always understood that. Joan was still young and a stranger to the world. She would love and be loved in all ways. He would never love like that again. There was never a day when his wife was far from his thoughts and he could conjure her back into his vision within seconds. In a single day he became a medium, always drifting in the lingering haze between worlds. When he eventually passed away too, some thirty years later, he smiled like a young boy returning home again after a long summer away.

"What do you want to say?" Ffiona prompted.

"I was sorry for your dad."

"Do you mean that?"

"I did love him once, didn't I? Maybe I still do, in some recess, some ventricle. I was sorry for him."

Ffiona stared ahead and smoothed her dress out on her legs. They finished their teas and waited, not sure if they could leave or not. Who could ever be sure about leaving? Ffiona was the first to move in the end, rising and collecting the mugs, before going back into the kitchen. The subtle wind brought down more rowan berries like sharp, red hail. They rolled down the slight slope in the lawn towards the flowerbed and Joan's eyes tracked them back to the forget-me-nots.

"Dad?" she said, before blushing and looking to make sure Ffiona hadn't heard.

It wasn't the same, of course. How could it be? Her father had loved her mother more than anything in this world, perhaps more than he loved Joan, in a way. Joan didn't feel that way about Gordon. He would have needed the diagnosis five years ago to elicit a similar reaction to that of her father. Yet she couldn't help but feel her soul shudder a little when she got the phone call. Her bones felt heavier.

"Jo?" Gordon said on the line.

"What?"

"Not even going to say hello?"

"The closest to 'hello' you'll get out of me is 'hell.'"

"Jo...I have to tell you something."

"Yeah?"

"I have cancer."

"…"

"Jo?"

"…"

"Joan?"

"Are you getting treatment?"

"The doctor says the best it'll do is prolong the inevitable."

"That's not what I asked."

"No. No, I'm not getting treatment."

"What about Fee?"

"I'm going to tell her tonight."

When Ffiona rang the doorbell at nine that night, Joan wrapped her daughter in her arms and rocked her. They moved together, shifting their weight from foot-to-foot and heaving tears. From afar, it looked like they were dancing.

In her chair in the garden, Joan watched Ffiona through the kitchen window washing their mugs. She got up and picked a few of the forget-me-nots. Bringing them inside, she set them down in the sink in front of her daughter. Then Joan took her hand. It was covered in soap and the heat of the water made her skin red. They stood there, watching the heads of the flowers float and circle each other in the ripples caused by the touch of Joan's fingers.

"When you see them, it means someone who isn't here is telling you that they love you," Joan said.

"Who is saying it?"

Joan pulled Ffiona into her arms and together they swayed to an invisible rhythm with the flowers. Neither spoke, not daring to venture an answer to the question that still hung in the air, but each certain of their own private reply.

# HERE'S

a secret: Rory McCullen was terrified of dying. It would happen any day now, he was sure of it. Though the fear came to him most nights, it wasn't on his mind at the moment. Currently, he was scanning the specials on the front of the restaurant's menu.

After he ordered, much to the bemusement of his friends, Rory took his Elvis Presley mug out of his satchel and placed it on the table in front of him. Raising a slow, shaking finger, he beckoned to the waiter who had already moved on to taking the others' orders.

"Yes?" the waiter asked.

"I'd like some milk too. In my mug, if you please," Rory said.

If the waiter was surprised he didn't show it, or at least Rory didn't notice, and he obliged as soon as he finished noting down the rest of the orders. Taking the gaudy mug with him, the waiter went off in search of some milk in the kitchen.

Rory didn't see his friends tut and exchange looks between themselves, which suggested silently that they wished he would show a little more decorum in public. The truth was that Rory simply didn't have any gauge for social awkwardness or poor etiquette whatsoever. Most people can detect cues that dictate how they ought to behave in a given situation, but this just wasn't a skill Rory ever learned. He lived in his own world, his existence only crossing over into reality in the moments when he thought he might die.

It was hard to say at what point Rory began to think so morbidly. He never felt especially in tune with life. Rory lived in the space between the two glass plates of a double-glazed window; he saw the world, but couldn't touch it. His skin frosted with breath and traces of other people, but he remained out of reach, always on the other side of some invisible partition.

Perhaps it would have been easier for Rory to maintain a grip on serenity if he lived with someone else. The world was a lonely place for an old man to spend his final years. It wasn't a lack of common sense that prevented him from supressing these dark thoughts – he knew that death was a statistical guarantee – but it was an intrusive shadow that ate away at the sunshine of all his days. Another soul could split a burden such as this, but Rory had only ever been in love once and that was a long time ago. Her name was Simone.

The waiter returned with the Elvis Presley mug as full of milk as he could manage without spilling it as he carried it back to Rory. It wasn't until Rory took his first sip that he realised he didn't know what the waiter looked like. He never raised his eyes to his face. That happened sometimes when he was speaking to someone. He would simply forget to look at them.

"Your eyes are like buoys," Simone said. "They're stuck in place, but still drifting up and down, up and down, never resting, never really a fixture of the sea."

She said lots of things that Rory didn't really understand and this was one of them. It was more the *way* she said it that intrigued him. Always with her dark curls bowing into her heart-shaped face, that broad forehead and pointed chin, and a smile so delicate that it may as well not be there at all. He saw her in parts like that, but unable to take in her whole appearance at once, as though he could only have a piece of her at a time.

His friends at dinner were speaking about the news. Rory sat at the head of the table, with the two sets of couples on either of the longest sides. On his right, Rose was growing animated as she explained the story. She wore three thick, gold bangles on her left wrist and they clanged against everything. Her enthusiastic gesticulations were punctuated by the reverberations of gold on gold, or the sharp knock of the metal on the wooden table. As she spoke, it was hard to take his eyes off her mouth, which was framed with the brightest lipstick Rory had ever seen in his life. It was so colourful, that it was easy to notice where it had seeped beyond the outline of her lips into the subtle wrinkles around them as tiny scarlet veins, no wider than hairs.

"But did you hear *why* he did it?" Rose said, her bangles smacking together. "They say his wife –"

"She left him!" Andrew, her husband, finished.

"Excuse me, you brute. *I* was telling it. Yes, she left him. Took the children and –"

"And ran off to her mother's place in Dorset. Dorset of all places!"

"Andrew! Right. She left him because he –"

"Well he was obviously unhinged now, wasn't he?"

"Right, you nuisance, why don't *you* tell it?" Rose snapped at Andrew. "Go on, finish the story."

"Okay, yes, well…well actually that's it, isn't it?"

"Yes. Yes that is *it*. Absolutely typical. I wish you'd run off to bloody Dorset."

They bickered constantly. They interrupted, snapped at, and insulted the other one all the time. The sound of the other person's voice was like a knife screeching across a plate. But they had been dedicated to this argument for decades upon decades. Rory often thought that they must love each other – really, *really* love each other – to find the other person that irritating and still be willing to put up with them for upwards of forty years.

Unlike his wife who was surprisingly energetic for her age, Andrew was slower and more deliberate in his movements. His thin face was topped by a balding scalp, which he blamed entirely on Rose.

"I'd still have my luscious locks if I hadn't married a bleedin' banshee," he always said. "The sound of her nagging alone made it all seize up at the roots and drop dead."

Andrew's appearance was as striking as his wife's in one regard; his eyes were like sea glass. In certain lighting they appeared almost clear, with only the vaguest hint of an aquamarine glow. It gave him an intimidating air, eclipsing every expression with a cold, sharp stare that he didn't intend, but had nonetheless.

The other couple at the table was Leonard and Anita. In many ways, they were the opposite of Andrew and Rose. Their relationship was smooth. In all the years Rory knew them, he never once heard them argue or so much as disagree. Despite this, it was Andrew and Rose who seemed closer, each knowing the other so well that, regardless of their endless disagreements, they could predict their thoughts, words, and actions without the slightest bit of effort. On the other hand, Leonard and Anita were more conversational, taking turns while talking and eagerly listening to what the other had to say as though it was all brand new, as though they were soaking in their love for the first time.

"I just can't understand how a person could do something like that," Anita said.

She shifted uncomfortably in her chair, both from the subject matter and from the back support cushion she brought with her, which was proving useless against the restaurant's shapeless, bolt-upright seating. All it appeared to be doing was pushing her back too far forwards, creating the opposite problem to the one she was trying to solve. Leonard leaned over and tried to adjust it for her as he spoke.

"He was not of sound mind," Leonard said.

"No, dear. You're right. A terrible thing."

"Terrible."

When Leonard was done trying to help his wife, he kissed the top of her head, upon which the shape of her hair vaguely resembled dandelion seeds. Then he smiled at Anita, flashing a set of excellent, albeit false, teeth. Everyone nodded as the conversation concluded, like the topic was as inconsequential as the weather and, to them, it was. Only Rory failed to acknowledge what was happening, letting the conversation pass over him like a breeze tousling the remaining strands of hair on his sun-spotted scalp. He took another swallow of milk and thought of Simone again.

She wouldn't look like she did in his memory if she were present tonight. No, she would look better. A real, older woman here and now beat any youthful visage that lingered in his mind, untouchable, unkissable, and entirely lost to him. He tried to picture her face not as it was, but as it could be, skin slightly dulled, lines forming cosy parentheses around every smile, but her eyes still the colour of topaz.

Simone would always know what to do. Her manners were pristine. She wouldn't be caught dead drinking milk out of a novelty mug in the middle of a restaurant. Rory wondered why people said "wouldn't be caught dead." The dead don't get caught doing anything. They don't drink milk. The redundancy of the idiom entertained him while the waiter returned with the appetisers. If anyone could get away with his terrible table manners, it would be Simone.

People just loved her in a way that nobody loved him. It didn't bother Rory. She filled every room she stepped into with light and plastered smiles onto faces wherever she went, even when her own was small and secretive. When Rory walked into a room, people rolled their eyes. If a sigh could be embodied in a single person, it was Rory. He was exasperation personified.

"How's your camembert, dear?" Anita asked Leonard, readjusting her cushion for a moment.

"Lovely, darling. And your melon?"

"Sweet as you."

"I can't believe you ordered fish for a starter," Rose said to Andrew, her bangles sliding up and down her arm.

"What's wrong with fish?"

"You ordered plaice for your main. Fish *and* fish."

"I'd expect fish to go very well with more fish."

"It's too much."

"Oh, dear, you have to try this," Leonard said, cutting off a piece of his baked cheese and placing it delicately onto the edge of his wife's plate.

"Wow," Anita said as she ate it. "Now that is excellent."

"Too much fish? The cheek! It's the same amount of food as the rest of you are having," Andrew said.

"Have a little variety! You've never been adventurous," Rose said.

"I like what I like."

"This milk is great," Rory said, and the two couples stopped to stare at him as he took another swig before tucking into his escargots.

"Rory...milk and *snails?*" Andrew said.

For once, all four of his friends were in complete agreement as they nodded and struggled to look away from Rory, who slipped them into his mouth in between gulps of his staple beverage. Rose pressed her lips together so tightly that for a second her lipstick couldn't be seen at all. Andrew's piercing eyes blinked rapidly.

"They're very garlicky. The milk cuts through it. Like a palette cleanser. Brilliant stuff."

"Do you think...may I try one?" Anita asked. "I've always wanted to, but I've never been brave enough. I think of the ones on the garden wall and get all nervous."

Rory nudged one onto her plate with a knife. Anita poked at it cautiously as though it might spring back to life at any moment, if snails ever sprang in the first place. Then she took a little breath, stabbed it, and shoved it into her mouth with her eyes squeezed shut.

"Oh blimey, it *popped!*" she cried.

"What?" Leonard enquired, with his perfect grin.

"There was...resistance when I bit it. It compressed and then sort of gave way. A pop!"

"Flaming Nora. And what does it taste like?"

"Like garlic. And butter. They must be like sponges and just soak up whatever you cook them in. And you know what?" Anita paused. "I could really go for a glass of milk right about now."

Rory waved the waiter over for a refill in his mug and an extra serving of milk for his friend. The waiter smiled and did as he was asked.

The rest of the meal went on in a similar way, Leonard and Anita sharing food and smiles, Andrew and Rose swapping ferocity and scowls, and Rory daydreaming to himself between mouthfuls. After it was over, Andrew and Rose gave him a lift back to his house as Leonard and Anita had been the ones to pick him up.

"Slow down, Andy," Rose said.

"Don't you start, woman," Andrew sighed.

"You're tearing down this road like Evel sodding Kneivel."

"I'm going the speed limit."

"The speed limit of what? The Autobahn?"

Then, from the back seat, Rory caught Andrew's lips twitch and his hard eyes soften in the rear view mirror.

"You make me mad, Rose. Absolutely hopping."

"You love it."

"I bloody well do not," he said, but he took one of his hands off the wheel long enough to stroke her leg. She covered his with one of hers, her jewellery rattling in the dark car.

They began arguing again not even thirty seconds later until they reached Rory's house. He thanked them both for the lift and the good evening. If Simone were here, coming home would be the best part of any night. As it stood now, it was the worst.

Rory thought of his hands around her waist like he did every time he put the key in the lock. In the seconds between inserting the key and opening the door, he relived the hours of their first night together. All the fumbling, the giggling because they both had too much scotch at the Christmas party, her in that blue dress, blue like the sea at midnight, blue like the festive lights he strung up around the door, blue like all the dreams he thought could never become real... She sighed after he kissed her on the front steps, not that same sigh people usually gave him, but one of longing. A sigh to stop time.

They didn't go inside straight away. When the kiss they shared was over, he reached for her hands that were as frozen as the winter night and held them to his chest. Then he lowered his arms and put them around her, pulled her whole body to his as if to make them one person.

Alone, he opened the door and went inside, flipping the light switch on the wall next to him as he locked up. As he made his way to the kitchen to wash his Elvis mug, he edged his way around the stacks of magazines that stood like pillars in the middle of his front room. Every copy of *Fisherman's World* since 1968.

In the kitchen, Rory sidestepped the pile of post by the back door and got to the sink, where dirty dishes were loaded high on top of the draining board. His Elvis mug was special though and needed washing, drying, and putting away. It had to be returned to the cabinet in the dining room with his other favourite things before he could go to bed. It belonged on the middle shelf between a pocket-sized clay bust of Ray Charles and a wristwatch in a box that was once Simone's. The time was stopped at forty three minutes past six.

He gave it to her as a present on their fifth wedding anniversary. By that time, he'd met Leonard and Andrew at work and befriended them both. They brought Anita and Rose over in the evening for a meal together to celebrate the occasion. Simone always preferred having people over and playing hostess instead of going out. Giving her home to others for a few hours filled her with joy like nothing else in the world.

The three couples spent the evening after they ate playing charades in the front room – magazine-free and spotless at the time – and sipping Baileys out of tiny crystal glasses.

"Those are ridiculous," Rory said when Simone pulled them out of their cardboard box.

"I know, but we never use them," she said, her dark hair falling into her face as she inspected them.

"Weren't they a wedding present?"

"I think so. From your aunt and uncle."

"Well, if we're ever going to make use of them, it may as well be tonight."

"They'll stop us having too much to drink, I suppose."

"Is that what you think?" he laughed.

Rory placed his clean mug back in the cabinet. He was about to touch the watch before closing the door, but didn't want to get his grubby fingerprints all over it.

It was a beautiful thing, he thought. Silver and slim. As elegant as Simone was in every way. She had the thinnest wrists, so small he could wrap his forefinger and thumb around each fully and with room to spare. When he bought the watch, he had to get four of the links removed just so it would fit – a measurement he figured out by cutting a length of string down to the size of one of her bracelets and carrying the string in his pocket to the jeweller's. Her wrists may have been tiny, but they were strong. All day Simone worked with her arms, lifting, cutting, carrying, moving, stirring, dusting, wiping, scrubbing… These were wrists that could withstand anything. Wrists like that deserved to be adorned with something beautiful.

He was tired now – being around other people no longer energised him like it used to – but couldn't go to bed. If he did,

Rory knew he'd start thinking about dying again. Instead, he went back to the front room to watch television.

The only things on this late were teleshopping, news, murder mysteries, and adult entertainment. Not feeling like seeing any of those in particular, Rory loaded up the motorcycle racing he'd recorded from that afternoon which came on while he was out having his daily walk. Rory wouldn't miss that walk for anything. It didn't matter if torrential rain was ripping the sky open. Rory went no matter what. It was a combination of wanting to try his best to keep his heart pumping as long as possible and an urge to get out of that house. Besides, he hated watching television in the middle of the day. If he did that, then there would be nothing to watch at night when he really needed to distract himself.

The thought always began with her face. *Your eyes are like buoys*, she said, and the vision of her would blur as Rory struggled to see the full picture of what she looked like. There would be her hair, her eyes, her skin, those wrists, but never all of her. God, how he wanted all of her. *They drift up and down*, she said, *up and down*, until it got so frustrating that he stopped being able to see anything at all. She would disappear from his mind as though stepping backwards from a streetlight into the shadows. *Never resting* and the motorcycles screamed through the speakers. *Never really a fixture of the sea*, blue like her dress that first night. Then everything would be blue, growing darker and darker until all Rory could see was black. Black was the void of colour. It was the emptiness of space. Black was death.

Rory knew he was going to die soon. His footing was shakier than it used to be and his hands trembled more. Fingers that once gripped with firm confidence now touched everything with uncertainty. Was he strong enough to pick that up? Could he manage to carry this? Would his shopping be too heavy today? The most difficult part was that he didn't *feel* old. As far as he was concerned, he was still twenty-five and full of life, potential, and all the possibilities of a future unlived. It was like how Leonard and Anita still spoke to each other with tenderness the way young lovers do, or how Andrew and Rose treated every argument like their first. Growing up was only body snatching. It comes like a thief in the dark. A person goes to bed in their mid-twenties and wakes up in their eighties, if they wake up at all. It was for this reason that Rory viewed the term "octogenarian" as a dirty slur. He was just barely on the cusp of adulthood. No one could ever be a fixture of this sea.

He must have fallen asleep at some point because he woke with a start a couple of hours after he turned on the television. Something about the way the motorcycles tore around the screen in circles made him dozy. Pushing himself up carefully onto his feet, Rory turned it off and weaved between the magazines to go upstairs. His bedroom was no different to the rest of the house.

Mountains of clothes gathered in every square foot of the floor. Shirts he hadn't seen in years lurked in the bottom layer, covered by ugly finds from thrift stores and street markets. Rory couldn't help himself. If anything caught his attention for even a second, he bought it. He knew how hard it was to steal his focus. Items that could were worth buying.

In bed, he stared at the ceiling in that way he loved to do, because it looked so clean and nothing littered its surface. That was another secret about Rory McCullen; he hated himself for his compulsion. Everywhere he looked he was reminded of time, and time made him think of death.

The stacks of magazines were nothing more to him than a physical measurement of all the years he lived. Every issue was indicative of his life clock running down, until one day a copy would arrive and it would be the last. He'd stop as still and as silent as Simone's watch. It was a three-dimensional bar chart in the middle of his living room. He ached to go back to his fifth wedding anniversary, playing charades with his wife and friends in a clean, welcoming home.

"Right, right, it's my turn," Rose said, taking one of the cards to silently act out.

She gestured to indicate: *film, seven words, second word*. Then Rose drew circles around the top of her head in the air and clasped her hands together in prayer. They began shouting guesses. *Angel! Praying! Christian! God! Jesus! Angel (we already did that one)! Good!* Rose clapped her hands. Yes, it was "good." She signed for the fourth word and acted the part of the Devil next, holding her fingers up to her temples like little horns and sticking her tongue out. *The Devil! Satan! Evil! Bad!* Rose jumped up and down. It was "bad." Then, slowly and with a huge grin on her face, she spun around and pointed a finger at her husband. *Ugly! The Good, The Bad, and The Ugly!* They all shouted at once, except for Andrew, who squeezed his dazzling eyes shut and pretended to sob into his Baileys. Then Rose gave him a noisy, dramatic kiss. Thankfully, she wasn't into wearing intense lipsticks at the time, or the pair of them would have ended up looking like they'd been smacked across the chops.

Rory smiled faintly as he looked up from his bed. That was the last night their friends got to see Simone. In the dark, he felt safe enough to admit to himself that it was the best time of his life. They finished the bottle of Baileys together in those stupid, miniature glasses and danced so badly to The Beach Boys that Leonard fell over, pulling Anita down with him. They all collapsed in fits of giggles. Everything that came after that was just waiting out the days.

It was the phone call that broke him.

On a warm evening in September, 1968, Rory was just taking the dinner out the oven when it came. Simone was working as a secretary back then and sometimes got held up. Rory didn't mind. In fact, he almost liked when she was late because it gave him the chance to cook. It was a task he revelled in, always looking for new recipes and tricks to try, but when Simone was home she did everything. It wasn't for a lack of offering a hand on his part, she just loved looking after people. On those rare days when Rory could repay the favour, he put in every ounce of effort he could. That evening, it was duck breast with all the trimmings and a bottle of a gorgeous red wine he was saving for no reason, the way people often do with wine. He answered the phone, expecting to hear her on the other end, but it was a man's voice.

Rory knew before the man said anything. He understood in the pause that followed the stranger's quivering voice as he introduced himself. Every answer to every question Rory had was given in that one breath. A fixture of the sea – his fixture – was gone. A ship wrecked on the side of the road. A vessel losing all its water to metal and glass.

They let him have her watch back, its hands frozen dead at the time when she was struck by the car on her walk home. Rory assumed it stopped from the impact, like if the battery got knocked loose, but remarkably there wasn't a scratch on it. The next day, the postman put a flyer for a subscription to *Fisherman's World* through the letterbox. Rory didn't think twice. He filled it out, making sure the date was clear in pristine black ink and block capitals. Even though it hadn't been twenty four hours yet, he was certain he couldn't keep counting the time between the present and her presence. The magazines counted for him, each symbolising another fortnight gone by until Rory could barely walk through his living room.

From his bed, he imagined what Simone's head would feel like on his chest, how she would draw lines across his stomach with her fingers, her hair tickling his neck as she nuzzled up to him. He felt his eyelids start to drop as his gaze moved down from the ceiling to the shape of his feet under the duvet. No matter how much time had gone by, he still couldn't bear to sleep on her side of the bed, so the lump his body made under his half of the sheets always looked small. His life was rich with friends and he was still loved, but in the dark he couldn't help but feel impossibly lonely, until the last moments of the day. In the final seconds, as Rory closed his eyes, he thought of keys turning in locks, buoys adrift in the sea, the clinking of crystal glasses, and slept.

# ACKNOWLEDGEMENTS

'Citroen Sid' appeared in Retreat West's anthology, *No Good Deed* (2019). 'These Arms' appeared in opia's inaugural issue, *Nostalgia* (2021), and contains lines from Otis Redding's song, 'These Arms of Mine.'

*All That Glisters* is dedicated to my grandparents, John and Ann. They taught me everything I know about how to be a good person and that, though I may not always succeed, what counts is the trying.

This book contains some of their love, jokes, and wisdom. May they bring you comfort.

LAY OUT YOUR UNREST